Dog Diary

Written by Mairi Mackinnon

Illustrated by Fred Blunt

How this book works

The story of **Dog Diary** has been written for you to read with your child. You take turns to read:

You read these words.

Today was fun.
First I woke up Jock.

I hid in a box,
and I bit a sock.

4

5

Your child reads these words.

You don't have to finish the story in one session. If your child is getting tired, put a marker in the page and come back to it later.

You can find out more about helping your child with this book, and with reading in general, on pages 30-31.

Dog Diary

Turn the page to start the story.

Today was fun.
First I woke up Jock.

I hid in a box,
and I bit a sock.

We had our breakfast
and went to work.

I sat in a van,
and I did not yap.

"All right, Pip,
now down you hop."

I met a cat, and
I did not nip.

"Good boy, Pip,
let's go to the park."

I ran and ran
in a big zig zag...

An open gate!
And what's that smell?

I ran up a hill, and
Jock had to yell.

A can of fizz?
I had a quick lick...

Time to go home,
or so I thought –

I got on a bus,
but Jock did not.

Ah yes, the van –
oh help, now what?

"No, Pip!
Quick, Pip!"

Off I got.

"Watch the puddle, Pip,
don't jump yet."

I fell in,
and I got wet!

"Bathtime and suppertime,
boy," Jock said.

I am back,
I am fed.

I let Jock
get to bed.

Puzzle 1

Read the sentences. Do you think Pip is being a good dog or a bad dog?

1.

I sat in a van,
and I did not yap.

2.

I met a cat,
and I did not nip.

3.

I ran up a hill,
and Jock had to yell.

4.

I let Jock
get to bed.

Why don't you talk about what Pip
dreams about when he is asleep?

Puzzle 2

Choose the right sentence for each picture.

1. I ran and ran.

2. I had a quick lick.

3. I hid in a box.

4. I am in bed.

A

B

C

D

Puzzle 3

Read the questions, and answer yes or no.

1.

Can Pip run?
Can Jock run?

2.

Is Pip on a bus?
Is Jock on a bus?

3.

Did Pip get wet?
Did Jock get wet?

Answers to puzzles

Puzzle 1

1.
2.
3.
4.

Puzzle 2

1. I ran and ran. - B
2. I had a quick lick. - C
3. I hid in a box. - A
4. I am in bed. - D

Puzzle 3

1. Yes, Pip can run.
   Yes, Jock can run.
2. Yes, Pip is on a bus.
   No, Jock is not on a bus.
3. Yes, Pip got wet.
   No, Jock did not get wet.

Guidance notes

Usborne Very First Reading is a series of
books, specially developed for children who are
learning to read. In the early books in the series,
you and your child take turns to read, and
your child steadily builds the knowledge and
confidence to read alone.

The words for your child to read in **Dog
Diary** introduce these eight letters or letter-
combinations:

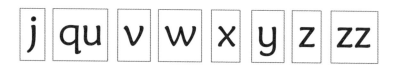

Your child will now be familiar with all the
letters of the alphabet – a major milestone
in learning to read. Later books in the series
gradually introduce more letter-combinations
and spelling patterns, while reinforcing the ones
your child already knows.

You'll find lots more information about the
structure of the series, advice on helping your
child with reading, extra practice activities and
games on the Very First Reading website,*
www.usborne.com/veryfirstreading

*US readers go to **www.veryfirstreading.com**

Some questions and answers

- **Why do I need to read with my child?**
  Sharing stories and taking turns makes reading an enjoyable and fun activity for children. It also helps them to develop confidence and reading stamina, and to take part in an exciting story using very few words.

- **When is a good time to read?**
  Choose a time when you are both relaxed, but not too tired, and there are no distractions. Only read for as long as your child wants to – you can always try again another day.

- **What if my child gets stuck?**
  Don't simply read the problem word yourself, but prompt your child and try to find the right answer together. Similarly, if your child makes a mistake, go back and look at the word together. Don't forget to give plenty of praise and encouragement.

- **We've finished, now what do we do?**
  It's a good idea to read the story several times to give your child more practice and more confidence. Then you can try reading **Bad Jack Fox** at the same level or, when your child is ready, go on to Book 5 in the series.

Edited by Jenny Tyler and Lesley Sims
Designed by Caroline Spatz

First published in 2010 by Usborne Publishing Ltd., Usborne House,
83-85 Saffron Hill, London EC1N 8RT, England. www.usborne.com
Copyright © 2010 Usborne Publishing Ltd.